Millie's Party

Titles in the Bunch:

Baby Bear Comes Home
Big Dog and Little Dog Visit the Moon
Clumsy Clumps and the Baby Moon
Delilah Digs for Treasure
Dilly and the Goody-Goody · Happy Sad
Horse in the House · I don't want to say Yes!
Juggling with Jeremy · Keeping Secrets
Mabel and Max · Magnificent Mummies
Midnight in Memphis · Millie's Party
Monster Eyeballs · Mouse Flute · The Nut Map
Owl in the House · Peg · Promise you won't be cross
Riff-Raff Rabbit · Rosie and the Robbers
Runaway Fred · Tom's Hats

First published in Great Britain 1999 by Mammoth
an imprint of Egmont Children's Books Limited
239 Kensington High Street, London W8 6SA
Published in hardback by Heinemann Library,
a division of Reed Educational and Professional Publishing Limited
by arrangement with Egmont Children's Books Limited.
Text copyright © Paul Stewart 1999
Illustrations © Bernard Lodge 1999
The Author and Illustrator have asserted their moral rights.
Paperback ISBN 0 7497 3248 2
Hardback ISBN 0 434 80142 9
10 9 8 7 6 5 4 3
A CIP catalogue record for this title is available from the British Library.
Printed and bound in Dubai at Oriental Press Limited.

Paul Stewart

Millie's Party

Illustrated by Bernard Lodge

BLue Bananas

For Anna
P.S.

For Katherine
B.L.

'It will be my birthday soon,' said Millie.

'Not long now,' said Mum. 'Would you

like to make your party list?'

'Yes, please!' said Millie. 'I'd like to ask Rosie, Tom, Hannah, Kate, Lily, Ben, Clyde, Rani, Sophie and Jo.'

6

Later that day Millie stood in the garden holding a letter.

Dear Sun,
you are invited
to my party.
Place: The Garden.
22 Beach Road.
Date: 21st April.
Time: 2 o'clock
to 5 o'clock.
Love from
Millie xxx

Millie climbed up the apple tree

and waited for a strong gust of wind.

When it came, she let go of the paper

and watched it fly away.

She was just about

to climb down

when she heard a voice.

Who's there?

It's me, Wind.

'It's not fair,' it said.

'You always invite Sun.

What's wrong with us?'

9

Millie felt she was going to fall.

But she didn't.

Instead, she flew up and up,

into the bright blue sky.

11

Millie landed with a bounce

on a fluffy cloud.

In front of her

floated four giants.

Who are you?

Guess!

Millie looked at

the huge roly-poly giant

with curly hair

and puffed-out cheeks.

If that was Wind, then the others
must be Fog, Rain and Snow.
'Every year we wait
for an invitation
to your party,'
said Rain.

'And every year you invite Sun instead,'

huffed Wind.

'So we've decided to hold

a competition,' said Fog.

'Whoever makes you laugh most
will be invited to your party.'

That sounds fun!

Are you ready?

15

Fog went first.

He swooped down

and covered the town in

a thick blanket of grey.

'What did you think of that?'

he asked, when he returned.

'I didn't see a thing,' said Millie.

'It was too foggy.'   Ho Ho Ho!

The other giants laughed at poor Fog.

Ha Ha Ha!

He He He!

When Wind hit town,

Millie saw it all.

Wherever Millie looked,

Wind was playing tricks.

whoo

He blew umbrellas
inside out. He snatched hats.

He slammed doors and pulled the washing from the lines. Millie couldn't help laughing.

Bang!

Then Wind hurried back
and asked the other giants,
'Did she laugh?'

'Only once,' said Rain.

'Now it's my turn.'

The sudden change in the weather
caught everyone by surprise.
Rain poured down and
people bumped into each other
as they ran for shelter.
This made Milly laugh.

It's torrential!

Soon the roads were like rivers . . . with boats floating on them! Millie laughed again. 'That was twice you laughed,' said Snow. 'My turn now.'

Everyone was pleased
when Snow fell.
Millie watched children
throwing snowballs.

They were all laughing
and Millie laughed too.

A boy fell off

his toboggan and Millie

laughed again.

A dog ran over and licked the boy's face.

Millie laughed again, even louder.

But Snow didn't know
when to stop. Soon everyone
was shivering cold.

Cars got stuck, pipes froze and
the milkman and the postman
couldn't get through.

Millie began to have doubts.

Suppose it snowed so hard that no one

could get to her party?

Snow came back in a flurry.

'You laughed three times at me,'

he said, 'so I'm the winner.

Now I will be coming

to your party.'

'We'll see about that,'

a friendly voice boomed.

And there was the biggest

giant of all – Sun.

Sun beamed down warm and strong.

'Don't worry, Millie,' he said. 'I'll make

sure your party is a good one.

Now climb on to

one of my sunbeams

and I'll take you home.'

When the day of the party arrived
it was warm and sunny. At two o'clock
the door bell rang. And there stood
Rosie, Tom, Hannah, Kate, Lily, Ben,
Clyde, Rani, Sophie and Jo.

Soon everyone was in the garden playing Hide and Seek.

When it was Millie's turn, she ran to the end of the garden to hide and a very strange thing happened . . .

Fog came and helped her to
hide so that no one
could find her.

When Millie came out

from her hiding place,

there was another surprise . . .

Big white flakes of snow were falling!

Snow sent just enough to build

a snowman, and everyone helped.

Then Sun came out again.

Mum carried the birthday cake into the

garden and everyone sang Happy Birthday.

Suddenly Wind arrived in a blustery gust to help Millie blow out all her candles in one go.

Wind made the balloons dance
and the tablecloth flap,
and juggled with the paper cups.
Then all was still again.

When the last crumb of
birthday cake was gone, the sky
began to get dark. Rain poured down,
making puddles everywhere. Millie and
her friends laughed as they
splashed their way up the
garden and into
the house.

When it was time to go home, everyone collected their coats and thanked Millie for a lovely party. Outside, Sun shone through the raindrops and made a beautiful rainbow in the sky.

Millie thought it was her best party ever.

She was so happy, she wrote a

thank you letter to the weather giants

for making her birthday so special.